Itham Forest Li

item by the last date sta

'ess required by anot

D1137398

The Tractor
Factor

WALTHAM FOREST LIBRARIES

904 000 00677110

'The Tractor Factor'
An original concept by Amanda Brandon
© Amanda Brandon

Illustrated by Maarten Lenoir

Published by MAVERICK ARTS PUBLISHING LTD
Studio 11, City Business Centre, 6 Brighton Road,
Horsham, West Sussex, RH13 5BB
© Maverick Arts Publishing Limited August 2020
+44 (0)1403 256941

A CIP catalogue record for this book is available at the British Library.

ISBN 978-1-84886-689-8

www.maverickbooks.co.uk

WALTHAM FOREST LIBRARIES	
904 000 00677110	
Askews & Holts	29-Sep-2020
JF FIR	
	L

This book is rated as: Orange Band (Guided Reading)
This story is mostly decodable at Letters and Sounds Phase 5.
Up to five non-decodable story words are included.

The Tractor Factor

by Amanda Brandon

illustrated by Maarten Lenoir

Scotty Sheepdog was polishing his red tractor. He watched the animals getting ready for the talent show.

There were dancing ducks, singing sheep and acrobatic cats.

Scotty loved his tractor.

"My tractor should be in the talent show,"

he said.

"A tractor is too noisy. It can't sing like me," said Miss Baa Baa.

"But..." said Scotty.

"A tractor is too clumsy. It can't juggle like us," said the hens. "We have the Eggs Factor."

"My tractor has big buttons and bouncy wheels. When I turn on the engine, it ROARS. There must be something it can do in the show," said Scotty.

But no one heard him. They were too busy.

The animals didn't see Fox sneak in.

He saw the prize cup and said,

"There will be only one winner

in this show – ME!"

The day of the show arrived.

The animals used a trailer as a stage.

One by one they jumped on and did

their acts.

When everyone was watching the show,

Fox saw his chance to grab the cup.

He untied the trailer and it started
to roll down the hill!

Scotty and his tractor raced to the rescue.

Scotty threw out his rope and hooked the stage. He pulled the trailer back.

It swung left and right.

The tractor did a wheel spin.

All the animals got mixed up.

The ducks tried to dance on stage but they landed on Bull's Big Band.

"Oooo," cried the audience.

Scotty and his tractor did a figure of eight.

The cartwheeling cats landed on top of

the band.

"Yikes!" panted the cats.

Scotty bounced over a rock.

Two hens flew through the air.

They landed on the cats –

and started juggling their eggs.

"Ahh!" cheered the audience.

Fox rubbed his paws. Everyone was watching the stage.

Sneaky Fox grabbed the cup, but
Scotty saw him in his tractor mirror.
"Oh no you don't!" yelled Scotty.
He roared after Fox.

The animals clung on tight.

Scotty flicked a rope around Fox.

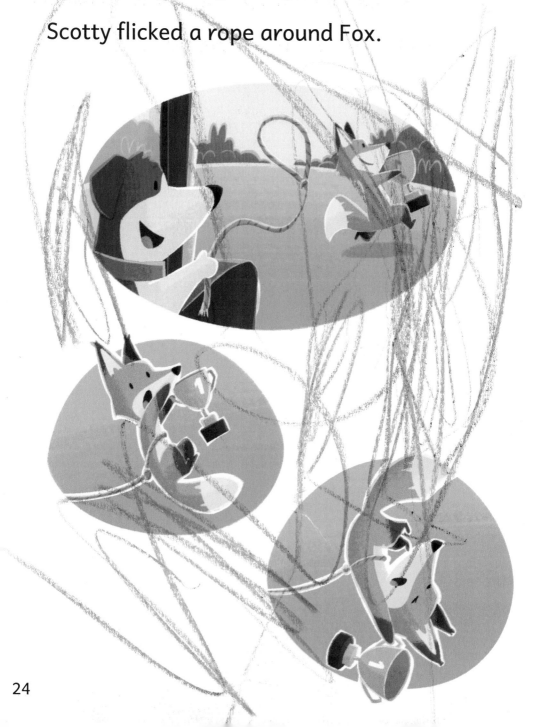

Fox flipped up... up... up... until **plonk!**

He landed on top of the pyramid.

The audience cheered.

"What a winner!" said Judge Cockerel.

He took the cup from Fox and gave it

to Scotty.

"Three cheers for Scotty," said the animals.

"He has got...

...the Tractor Factor!"

Quiz

1. What colour is Scotty's tractor?
a) Blue
b) Green
c) Red

2. Who has the Eggs Factor?
a) The goats
b) The hens
c) Scotty

3. Why does Fox untie the trailer?
a) To get the prize cup
b) To sing on the stage
c) To use Scotty's tractor

4. Fox flipped up... up... up... until _____!
a) Smash
b) Bang
c) Plonk

5. Who wins the talent show in the end?
a) The cats
b) Scotty
c) Fox

Book Bands for Guided Reading

The Institute of Education book banding system is a scale of colours that reflects the various levels of reading difficulty. The bands are assigned by taking into account the content, the language style, the layout and phonics. Word, phrase and sentence level work is also taken into consideration.

Maverick Early Readers are a bright, attractive range of books covering the pink to white bands. All of these books have been book banded for guided reading to the industry standard and edited by a leading educational consultant.

To view the whole Maverick Readers scheme, visit our website at

www.maverickearlyreaders.com

Or scan the QR code above to view our scheme instantly!

Quiz Answers: 1c, 2b, 3a, 4c, 5b